Karen's County Fair

**Look for these
and other books about Karen
in the
Baby-sitters Little Sister series**

1 *Karen's Witch*
2 *Karen's Roller Skates*
3 *Karen's Worst Day*
4 *Karen's Kittycat Club*
5 *Karen's School Picture*
6 *Karen's Little Sister*
7 *Karen's Birthday*
8 *Karen's Haircut*
9 *Karen's Sleepover*
#10 *Karen's Grandmothers*
#11 *Karen's Prize*
#12 *Karen's Ghost*
#13 *Karen's Surprise*
#14 *Karen's New Year*
#15 *Karen's in Love*
#16 *Karen's Goldfish*
#17 *Karen's Brothers*
#18 *Karen's Home Run*
#19 *Karen's Good-bye*
#20 *Karen's Carnival*
#21 *Karen's New Teacher*
#22 *Karen's Little Witch*
#23 *Karen's Doll*
#24 *Karen's School Trip*
#25 *Karen's Pen Pal*
#26 *Karen's Ducklings*
#27 *Karen's Big Joke*
#28 *Karen's Tea Party*
#29 *Karen's Cartwheel*
#30 *Karen's Kittens*
#31 *Karen's Bully*
#32 *Karen's Pumpkin Patch*
#33 *Karen's Secret*
#34 *Karen's Snow Day*
#35 *Karen's Doll Hospital*
#36 *Karen's New Friend*
#37 *Karen's Tuba*
#38 *Karen's Big Lie*
#39 *Karen's Wedding*
#40 *Karen's Newspaper*
#41 *Karen's School*
#42 *Karen's Pizza Party*
#43 *Karen's Toothache*

#44 *Karen's Big Weekend*
#45 *Karen's Twin*
#46 *Karen's Baby-sitter*
#47 *Karen's Kite*
#48 *Karen's Two Families*
#49 *Karen's Stepmother*
#50 *Karen's Lucky Penny*
#51 *Karen's Big Top*
#52 *Karen's Mermaid*
#53 *Karen's School Bus*
#54 *Karen's Candy*
#55 *Karen's Magician*
#56 *Karen's Ice Skates*
#57 *Karen's School Mystery*
#58 *Karen's Ski Trip*
#59 *Karen's Leprechaun*
#60 *Karen's Pony*
#61 *Karen's Tattletale*
#62 *Karen's New Bike*
#63 *Karen's Movie*
#64 *Karen's Lemonade Stand*
#65 *Karen's Toys*
#66 *Karen's Monsters*
#67 *Karen's Turkey Day*
#68 *Karen's Angel*
#69 *Karen's Big Sister*
#70 *Karen's Grandad*
#71 *Karen's Island Adventure*
#72 *Karen's New Puppy*
#73 *Karen's Dinosaur*
#74 *Karen's Softball Mystery*
#75 *Karen's County Fair*
#76 *Karen's Magic Garden*

Super Specials:
1 *Karen's Wish*
2 *Karen's Plane Trip*
3 *Karen's Mystery*
4 *Karen, Hannie, and
       Nancy: The Three
       Musketeers*
5 *Karen's Baby*
6 *Karen's Campout*

Little Sister

Karen's County Fair
Ann M. Martin

Illustrations by Susan Tang

A
LITTLE APPLE
PAPERBACK

SCHOLASTIC INC.
New York Toronto London Auckland Sydney

ISBN 0-590-69183-X

12 11 10 9 8 7 6 5 4 3 2 1   6 7 8 9/9 0 1/0

Printed in the U.S.A.   40

First Scholastic printing, July 1996

*The author gratefully acknowledges
Diane Molleson
for her help
with this book.*

1

Roses

"I love the smell of roses," I announced to my best friends Hannie and Nancy.

They nodded. The three of us usually like the same things.

It was the last day in June. We could see — and smell — roses everywhere. Red roses on the vine near the door of my house. Yellow roses across the street. Pink roses in my neighbor's yard.

Using my mother's special clippers, I carefully snipped a red rose from the vine. Then I snipped another and another. I

1

picked only the ones with perfect blossoms.

"Karen, are you sure it is all right to cut so many of your mother's flowers?" Nancy asked. She sounded worried.

"Mommy said we could," I reminded her.

"She said we could cut *some*," Hannie reminded me.

"Mmm," I said. I was hardly listening. I had to concentrate. I handed the flowers to Nancy. I needed both hands. One to hold the vine, the other to cut the roses that were harder to reach. *Snip. Snip. Snip.*

I wanted to put roses in every room in my two houses. I have a little house and a big house. Right now I was at the little house. But later that day, my brother and I would be going to the big house to spend the month of July with Daddy. (I will tell you more about my two houses later.) I also wanted enough flowers for Hannie and Nancy.

Snip. Snip.

"Karen!"

I looked up. Mommy was staring at us from the kitchen window. Actually, she was looking at her special rose bush. She did not seem very happy. Hmmm. Maybe I did get a little carried away.

I am Karen Brewer. I am seven years old. I have blonde hair, blue eyes, and a bunch of freckles. I wear glasses. I have two pairs. I wear the blue pair for reading. I wear the pink pair the rest of the time.

I adore roses. I also adore my best friends, Nancy Dawes and Hannie Papadakis. We do everything together. That is why we call ourselves the Three Musketeers. And guess what? Tomorrow the three of us are going to Farm Camp at Mrs. Stone's barn. My stepsister, Kristy, will be one of the counselors. Kristy is thirteen and a lot of fun.

"Karen," my mother repeated. "Are you ready to go to your father's? Have you packed your overalls for camp?"

I nodded. I had packed my overalls, my favorite sneakers, and a straw hat. (I might need the hat if we were out in the sun a lot.) Everything else I need is at Daddy's.

"Hannie, are you ready, too?" Mommy said.

"Yes, Mrs. Engel," Hannie answered. Hannie lives across the street from Daddy. We were going to drive her home.

"I picked enough roses for both my families," I told Mommy.

Mommy gave me a funny look. "Karen, you have enough flowers for the whole town of Stoneybrook." She smiled when she said that. Hannie and Nancy did, too.

2

I Am a Two-Two

"Can we stop for ice cream?" Andrew asked on the way to Daddy's. Andrew is my little brother. He is four going on five. He was sitting in the frontseat with Mommy. Hannie and I sat in back with the roses.

"Not today," Mommy answered.

"Please!" Andrew begged. "Puh-*lease*." (I think Andrew learned to say please that way from me.)

"Andrew," Mommy warned him. She gave him a Look.

Andrew quieted down.

Remember I told you I had two houses? Now I will tell you why.

A long time ago, when I was very little, I had one house and one family — Mommy, Daddy, Andrew, and me. We all lived in a big house in Stoneybrook, Connecticut. Then Mommy and Daddy started fighting — at first a little, then a lot. Finally, they got a divorce. They told us they still loved Andrew and me very much, but they did not love each other anymore. So, Daddy stayed in the big house. (It is the house he grew up in.) Mommy moved to a little house, not far away. Then Mommy married Seth. Now he is my stepfather. Daddy married again, too. He married Elizabeth, my stepmother.

Here is who is in my little-house family: Mommy, Seth, Andrew, me, Rocky and Midgie (Seth's cat and dog), Emily Junior (my very own rat), and Bob, Andrew's hermit crab.

Here is who is in my big-house family:

Daddy, Elizabeth, Andrew, me, Kristy, Charlie, Sam, David Michael, Emily Michelle, Nannie, Shannon, Boo-Boo, Goldfishie, Crystal Light the Second, Emily Junior, and Bob. (Emily Junior and Bob go back and forth when Andrew and I do.) Whew! Now you see why I needed to pick so many roses.

Kristy, Charlie, Sam, and David Michael are Elizabeth's children. (She was married once before, too.) That makes them my stepsister and stepbrothers. Charlie and Sam are old. They go to high school. David Michael is seven like me. Kristy is one of my favorite people. She runs the Babysitters Club with her friends from school. Emily Michelle is my adopted sister. (I love her very much. That is why I named my pet rat after her.) Daddy and Elizabeth adopted her from the faraway country of Vietnam. Emily is two and a half. Nannie is Elizabeth's mother. (That makes her my stepgrandmother.) She helps take care of the big house and all us kids. And the pets. We have a lot of them. Shannon is David Michael's puppy. Boo-Boo is Daddy's fat old cat. And Goldfishie and Crystal Light the Second are (guess what?) goldfish. Isn't it lucky Daddy's house is so big?

I made up special nicknames for my brother and me. I call us Andrew Two-Two and Karen Two-Two. (I thought up those names after my teacher read a book to our class. It was called *Jacob Two-Two Meets the Hooded Fang.*) Andrew and I are two-twos because we have two of so many things. We have two houses and two families, two mommies, two daddies, two cats, and two dogs. Plus, I have two bicycles, one at each house. (Andrew has two trikes.) I have two stuffed cats. Goosie lives at the little house. Moosie stays at the big house. Andrew and I have two sets of clothes, books, and toys. This way, we do not need to pack much when we go back and forth. I even have two pieces of Tickly, my special blanket.

And I have a best friend near each house. Hannie lives near Daddy. Nancy lives next door to Mommy.

So, you see, being a two-two is not too hard. Sometimes Andrew and I miss the family we are not staying with. But mostly we are very lucky. Think how many people love us.

"We're here!" Andrew called from the front seat. He rushed from the car into Daddy's arms. It took Hannie and me a little longer to get out of the car with all of our roses.

"Oh, you shouldn't have," Daddy and Elizabeth said together when they saw the flowers. (Daddy grows roses, too.) But I know he was happy to receive mine. So was Elizabeth. Even Sam and Charlie liked getting roses. Do you know anyone who doesn't?

3

Oliver Twist

"Moosie," I said to my stuffed cat the next morning, "how do I look?" Moosie stared at me from his pillow. He did not answer, of course. But I knew he thought I looked fine.

This is what I was wearing for my first day of Farm Camp: overalls, a blue-and-white striped T-shirt, red sneakers, and a bright green bandanna in my hair.

"Karen, are you ready?" Kristy called from downstairs.

"Almost!" I shouted back. I shoved some

clothes under my bed to make my room look neater. It was still a mess. But I did not want to be late.

I ran downstairs. Charlie was going to drive Kristy, Hannie, and me to camp in his gigundoly cool car. He calls it the Junk Bucket. I climbed in the backseat with Hannie, and we were on our way.

The Stones' farm is in Stoneybrook. But it is the part of Stoneybrook that looks like the country, the part where you can see lots of fields and cows. "Make a left turn here," I told Charlie after we passed the cemetery. (I have been to the farm before.)

"Karen, we know," Kristy said. But she was smiling.

Charlie pulled up by the rusty old tractor near the barn. I was the first one out of the car. "Come on, Hannie," I said. "Let's go find Nancy."

We found Nancy looking at some chickens. They were strutting around the yard. "Oh, they are so cute!" Nancy said. "I wonder if Mrs. Stone would let us hold one."

"Hey, Karen! You look like a farm boy in your overalls," a voice behind us called.

I groaned. The voice belonged to Bobby Gianelli. He goes to school with Hannie, Nancy, and me. And he is a gigundo pest — sometimes.

"Let's ignore him," Hannie suggested. I thought that was great idea. At least the other campers seemed nice. They were Cordelia, Charlotte, Sophie, Gregg, Gemma, Pamela, Ricky, and Chris. Guess what? Pamela, Chris, and Ricky go to school with us. We are all in Ms. Colman's second-grade class at Stoneybrook Academy. (Ricky is my pretend husband. We were married on the playground at school one day.) Sophie, Gregg, and Gemma were in my gymnastics class. Charlotte lives near the big house. Kristy sometimes baby-sits for her. The only camper I did not know was Cordelia. She looked younger than the rest of us. But that is all right. I knew Farm Camp was going to be fun, even with Mr. Pest.

First, Mrs. Stone gave us a tour of the farm. She showed us her gigundoly cool vegetable garden. There were rows and rows of carrots, radishes, lettuce, cabbages, tomatoes, and other plants I did not recognize. Mrs. Stone said they were herbs.

"You mean like parsley, sage, and mint?" Charlotte said. (Charlotte acts like a grown-up. Maybe that is because she is eight.)

"Yes," Mrs. Stone answered.

"Parsley, gross!" Bobby said. (We ignored him.)

Inside the barn we saw the animals. We met horses, pigs, more chickens, a goat, and best of all, a lamb. A soft, fuzzy lamb. Mrs. Stone told us his name was Oliver Twist, Ollie for short. He was named after the orphan, Oliver Twist. (Oliver Twist is from a book by a famous author called Charles Dickens.) And do you know why he was named that? Because Ollie is an orphan, too.

I felt sorry for Ollie. It must be awful not

to have any parents. I could not stop looking at the little lamb. He followed Mrs. Stone everywhere. Sometimes he butted her.

"Lambs butt their mothers to make them produce more milk," Mrs. Stone explained. "Ollie does it because he wants his bottle. I am trying to get him to eat other food. So I only give him one bottle each day."

"How old is Ollie?" I asked.

"He was born in April. He is almost three months old now."

I could have played with Ollie all day. But Mrs. Stone wanted to tell us about camp. Kristy and the other counselor, Mallory Pike, led us outside. (Mallory is eleven. She is in the Baby-sitters Club with Kristy.)

Outside, we gathered around Mrs. Stone. We sat under a big oak tree. I knew it was an oak tree because it had acorns.

Mrs. Stone told us the county fair was coming to Greenvale. Greenvale is a town near Stoneybrook. And guess what? We would spend the whole last day of camp at the fair.

"All right!" Bobby and Ricky said together. The rest of us cheered.

"There will also be contests at the fair," said Mrs. Stone.

"What kinds of contests?" Charlotte asked.

"Contests for handiwork, baking, and produce," Mrs. Stone answered. "You can choose which contest you would like to enter. You will need to complete a needlework project for the handicraft contest, work on a recipe for the baking contest, or raise vegetables for the produce contest."

"I want to grow vegetables," Bobby said.

"You do not have to decide right away," Mrs. Stone told him. "While you are at camp, you will all help take care of the animals. You will start a garden of your own, learn arts and crafts, and sing songs, too."

I looked at Hannie and Nancy. We smiled

at each other. Farm Camp sounded gigundoly cool.

Just then Ollie came out of the barn. I
think he was looking for Mrs. Stone. I ran
to pet him some more. I think I am in love
— with a lamb.

Tia

Old MacDonald had a farm
E-I-E-I-O
And on that farm he had some ducks
E-I-E-I-O

I sat with Emily in the family room. I was trying to teach her some songs.

"Eee Eeeee," Emily squealed.

"No, Emily. It's E-I-E-I-O."

"Eeeeeeeee," Emily shouted.

I sighed and put her on my lap. I decided to tell her about Farm Camp instead.

We had been going to camp for three days now. They had been three of the best days of my life.

Every morning we met in the barn. First, we fed and brushed the animals. I took care of Ollie. That day I had even given him his bottle. The other campers fed the chickens, horses, and goat. (I do not know why anyone even bothers to feed that goat. He eats everything he sees. He even ate the sheets Mrs. Stone hung on the line to dry.)

Next, we worked in our vegetable garden. We had already planted tomatoes, lettuce, carrots, and radishes. We learned that tomatoes grow above the ground on vines. Lettuce grows on the ground. And carrots and radishes grow under the ground. Mrs. Stone said we could take the vegetables home with us when camp was over. (It is a good thing everyone in my two families likes salad.)

After gardening, we helped Mrs. Stone with the cooking. That day we had made cornbread from scratch. (We taste everything we make. If it is good, we lick the bowls.)

Then we went to the sewing room. It is really a big study where Mrs. Stone keeps her sewing machine and her fabric. So far, we have learned how to mark fabric and cut it in a straight line. We also learned how to thread a needle. Well, I already knew how. But Bobby and Pamela did not. They kept pricking their fingers and complaining.

Mrs. Stone wanted us to choose which contest to enter in the fair. I was not sure which to choose. I liked working outside in the garden. (So did Hannie.) I also liked to cook, and taste everything. But best of all, I liked taking care of Ollie.

"What should I do, Emily?" I asked.

"Eeeee," Emily squealed again. I shook my head. Emily is very cute. But she is not easy to talk to.

"Karen, telephone," Nannie called from the kitchen.

"Hello," I said when I picked up the phone.

"Hello, Karen, it is Tia."

"Tia!" I shouted. Tia is my friend from Nebraska. I met her when I was visiting Granny and Grandad. She is seven, too. "Tia, I cannot believe it is you."

"It is me," Tia said, laughing.

Tia had some bad news and good news. Her bad news was that she was not going to Texas to visit her aunt and uncle. She was sad about that. The good news was her parents said that instead she could go to Stoneybrook to visit me. This was very exciting. But first I had to ask Daddy and Elizabeth about that.

"Daddy, Elizabeth! It is Tia. She wants to come to Stoneybrook. Please say yes. Please, please."

"Indoor voice, Karen," Daddy said. "Of course Tia is welcome." First Daddy talked to Tia's parents. Then Elizabeth talked to them. They worked everything out. Tia would visit for three weeks! Daddy and I would pick her up at the airport on Saturday. I could not wait.

5

Karen Brewer,
Lamb Trainer

I sat under Mrs. Stone's oak tree. I was brushing Ollie. His wool felt very soft.

"Karen," Kristy called. "Mrs. Stone wants to make an important announcement. We are meeting in the kitchen."

"Okay," I called. Ollie followed me to the kitchen door. But I could not let him in. Ollie is not allowed in the kitchen.

"Good morning, girls and boys," said Mrs. Stone.

"Mrs. Stone," I said, raising my hand. "I have a friend coming to visit me. Would it be okay if she came to camp?"

"Just a moment, Karen," Mrs. Stone said. "I would like to make my announcement first." Mrs. Stone continued, "You must choose your groups today. You will begin your projects next week."

Boo and bullfrogs. I still could not decide.

"Now, what did you want to ask me, Karen?" said Mrs. Stone.

I asked if Tia could come to Farm Camp with me.

"Yes," Mrs. Stone answered. "Tia can also join a group."

"She would like that," I said. "She lives on a farm in Nebraska. I do not want her to be homesick."

"Oh, Mrs. Stone," Bobby interrupted. "I want to be in the cooking group."

"That is fine, Bobby," Mrs. Stone answered. Kristy was carrying a big pad of paper. She wrote Bobby's name under Cooking Group.

"I thought you wanted to grow vegetables," I said.

"I changed my mind. Brownies taste better than carrots," said Bobby.

Ricky, Pamela, and Cordelia wanted to cook, too. Hmm, it would be fun to be in Ricky's group.

"Karen, join the sewing group with me," said Nancy. "Gregg and Gemma are in it, too."

"I like to sew," I said. "But I also like to garden."

Hannie wanted to work outside in the produce group. So did Charlotte and Chris. Everyone knew what they wanted to do — except me. (Sigh.) I wished I could decide.

Just then Ollie came to the kitchen window. He pressed his nose against the glass. Everyone laughed. I went to the window to talk to him. Suddenly I had a brilliant idea.

"Hey," I exclaimed. "Don't people enter lambs in livestock contests?" I did not wait for an answer. I knew they did. I once saw a state fair on TV.

"You want to enter Ollie in the livestock contest?" Kristy asked.

I nodded. "That can be my project."

Mrs. Stone and Kristy did not seem too happy about my idea. "Karen," Mrs. Stone said. "Ollie is a wonderful lamb, but he is not a show lamb. He has never been properly trained."

"I can train him," I insisted.

"It is not that simple," Mrs. Stone said. "You do not have much experience working with lambs. And Ollie is already three months old. Most animals begin training as soon as they are born. Entering an animal in a contest is a serious project, Karen. It takes a lot of time and effort."

Kristy agreed with Mrs. Stone. She reminded me about the livestock contest we saw on TV. "The kids you saw spent hours every day with their animals. They fed them, groomed them, and taught them how to behave."

"I can spend hours each day with Ollie," I said.

26

"Well, all right, Karen," Mrs. Stone finally said. "I see you are determined. But this means you will be in a group by yourself."

"That is all right," I said. I was thrilled. I ran outside to give Ollie a hug. "Ollie," I whispered. "We are going to win the blue ribbon."

At Camp

"I think we should grow tomatoes for the fair," said Charlotte.

"But the lettuce is growing better," Hannie pointed out.

"That is true," I said. "The lettuce looks better."

"Karen," Chris said. "You are not in the produce group. Hannie, Charlotte, and I can decide — without you."

I walked away in a huff. At least I had Ollie to keep me company. (And he was a lot nicer than Chris Lamar.)

I had already given Ollie his morning bottle. (Mrs. Stone had said I could feed him from now on.) Ollie gulped down his milk in no time. I thought about feeding him more. I want him to look big and healthy for the fair.

Next, Ollie and I played follow-the-leader. I was the leader, and Ollie followed me everywhere. He even wanted to follow me into the house when I visited the other groups. But I did not let him.

First, I went to the sewing room to see Nancy. She sat at a big table with Sophie, Gemma, Gregg, and Kristy. (Kristy was not going to sew. She was just helping them get started.) Guess what. Everyone wanted to make something different. Sophie and Gemma wanted to sew a pillow in the shape of a rabbit. Gregg wanted to make a beanbag cat. Nancy wanted to sew a baby quilt.

I liked the idea of a baby quilt the best. Especially if it had a lamb on it. But no one asked me what I thought.

Kristy wanted to know if I had practiced putting a halter on Ollie.

"Why would I do that?" I asked.

"To see if he will let you lead him," Kristy explained. "At the fair, you will probably have to lead him around a ring on a leash."

"Oh," I said. I was busy looking at a book of baby quilts.

I pointed to a pattern called Lambie Pie. It showed a lamb surrounded by tulips and butterflies. "I like this one," I said.

"I like the one with the teddy bear," said Nancy.

"There's one with a train," said Gregg. Soon Gemma and Sophie wanted to see the book, too. "These quilts are cuter than the rabbit pillows," said Gemma.

"Especially the one with the lamb on it," I repeated. But no one heard me. I decided to see what the kitchen group was doing. I could probably help them. (I am a very good cook.)

I found Bobby, Ricky, Pamela, and Cordelia making brownies with Mallory. They were putting a big tray of them in the oven. "We are going to win the contest with this recipe," said Bobby.

"Your brownies are not baked yet," I said. "How do you know how they will taste?"

"I just know," said Bobby. "They have a lot of chocolate in them."

"And nuts," Cordelia added.

They did sound good. I put my finger in the bowl and tasted the chocolate frosting. "Mmmm," I said.

"Hey, Karen!" Bobby exclaimed. He grabbed the bowl. "Only people in the cooking group can taste the frosting."

"The judges are not in your group," I said. "And if you want my honest opinion, I think you need to add more sugar." ("If you want my honest opinion" was something Charlie and his friends said. I thought it sounded very grown up.)

Bobby was not impressed. "Karen, leave us alone," he said.

Ricky and Cordelia thanked me. They are

31

much more polite than Bobby.

As soon as I walked outside, Ollie trotted over to me. I spent the rest of the morning brushing him. (I promised him I would brush him every day.) His coat looked soft and fluffy when I was done.

"Ollie, I want you to look perfect for the fair," I said. Ollie did not answer. Instead, he butted me.

"Oh, Ollie, are you hungry?"

Ollie butted me again. So I gave him another bottle. I did not want Ollie to starve. I hoped Mrs. Stone didn't mind.

7

A Trip to the Airport

The next morning, I woke up very early. I did not want to keep Tia waiting.

"Daddy," I said at breakfast. "Should we leave for the airport now?"

"Karen," Daddy answered. "We do not have to leave for two hours."

"Two hours." I groaned. "What will I do for two hours?"

Nannie and Elizabeth had a lot of ideas about what I could do. First I cleaned my room. That was Elizabeth's idea. Then Nannie and I made cupcakes for Tia. I decorated them with pink and white icing and sprinkles. Finally it was time to leave for the airport.

Kristy, Andrew, and David Michael decided to go with us. I was happy David Michael came. Andrew is not such a pest when David Michael is with him.

We arrived half an hour before Tia's plane.

"Let's look around the airport," I suggested. I had been to the airport many times. I knew there was a lot to see. First, we looked in a toy store. Then, we watched the planes take off and land. Soon, we heard Tia's flight announced over the intercom.

Daddy and Kristy sat in plastic chairs to wait. But Andrew, David Michael, and I were too excited. We walked around the aisles and looked out the window. We saw Tia's plane land. Then we saw a girl with very short dark hair walk off the plane. She was with a stewardess.

"She's here!" I cried. I rushed over to the gate.

"Tia!" I shouted.

"Karen," Tia called back. We ran into each other's arms and hugged. Then I introduced Tia to Daddy, Kristy, and David Michael. (Tia had met Andrew before.) She knew all about my two families. And they knew all about her.

Tia and I sat in the backseat and talked all the way home. I told her about Farm Camp and Ollie. Tia looked out the window a lot. She stared at all the stores and restaurants we passed. She loved downtown Stoneybrook. "Oh, Karen, there are so many neat-looking stores here."

"This is the town part of Stoneybrook," I explained. "The country part where we go to camp is nicer." Tia did not answer. She was too busy looking out the window.

When we arrived at the big house, Elizabeth, Nannie, Sam, and Shannon were there to meet us. Shannon bounded up to Tia. She licked her hand.

Elizabeth and Nannie hugged Tia and welcomed her to Stoneybrook. Sam carried her suitcase upstairs. Tia was going to sleep in the guest room near my room.

Tia started to unpack. But I stopped her. I wanted to show her around the house before lunch. I knew that would take a long time because Daddy's house is very big. It has three floors and nine bedrooms. Tia loved the whole house.

"Oh, Karen, you have a TV and a VCR," she exclaimed. "And air-conditioning."

"Well, yes." I said. (Tia does not have those things on her farm in Nebraska.)

"Karen, Tia," Kristy called. "Lunch-time!"

For lunch, we had tuna fish sandwiches, potato chips, pickles, fresh strawberries, and the special cupcakes.

Tia said they were the prettiest cupcakes she had ever seen. She also loved the potato chips. "We never have these at home," she said, munching happily.

"You know, Tia, these are fresh strawberries. We bought them at a farm in Stoneybrook."

Tia nodded and reached for another chip.

After lunch, I took Tia around the neighborhood. "Could we walk to the stores from here?" Tia asked.

"Well, no," I said. "Besides, it is too nice a day to spend inside a store." Instead I showed Tia our backyard and Daddy's big garden. "Daddy lets me help him with his roses," I said proudly. "We can both help him while you are here."

Tia did not answer. Next we walked to a nearby park. We sat on a bench and looked at the people walking their dogs. (Most of the dogs were poodles.) I told Tia about Mrs. Stone's animals.

"You have to meet Ollie," I said. "He is the best lamb." Instead of answering, Tia yawned. She was probably tired after her trip.

Strawberries, Peaches, and Plums

Tia really was tired. She went to bed right after dinner. She said that was her regular bedtime.

But guess what? Tia woke up before any of us and fed Shannon and Boo-Boo. So Shannon and Boo-Boo did not wake us up as they usually do. Daddy and Elizabeth were very happy. So was I.

Today was Tia's first full day in Stoney-brook. I wanted to make it special. I even had a plan. I had already talked it over with Daddy.

And at breakfast, I told it to Tia. "Tia," I said, "we are going to have a picnic — just you, me, Hannie, and Nancy. We are going to spend the whole day outside." It was a clear sunny day with puffy white clouds and a blue sky.

Tia smiled. But she did not seem too excited. Maybe she was tired from getting up so early.

After breakfast, Tia and I packed lunch.

"I know a wonderful place where we can have a picnic," I told Tia. "The backyard."

We sat under the big tree and spread out our blanket. Andrew and David Michael were in the backyard, too. They were playing catch. But they did not bother us, thank goodness.

I bit into a strawberry. "If I could be a fruit, I would be a strawberry," I said. "They are my favorite."

"I would be a plum," said Nancy. "I love the color."

"I would be a peach," said Hannie.

Tia was giving us a funny look. I think

she was trying not to laugh. "What fruit would you be?" I asked her.

"I don't know," she answered. "Maybe a banana." She did not seem too interested in fruit.

After we had cleaned up our picnic, Hannie wanted to go wading. I wanted to take a walk. Nancy wanted to play Frisbee. Tia was the only one who wanted to go indoors.

"There is nothing to do inside," I said.

"Couldn't we watch TV or rent a video?" Tia suggested. "It is so hot out here."

"Well, if you are hot, maybe we should go wading." I said.

"Yes!" Hannie said. She could not wait to go splashing in the brook near Daddy's house. The water only comes up to our knees.

"Let's change into our bathing suits," I said.

Hannie went home to get her suit. Nancy borrowed my ruffled peach suit. "Now you look like a peach," I said.

Nancy giggled.

We spent the rest of the afternoon wading in the brook. The water was warm and clear. We could see sand and pebbles underneath the water. Tia saw a frog. (It hopped away when the rest of us looked.)

I found a ladybug with ten dots on her back. "That means she is ten years old," I told the others. "Did you know a ladybug grows a new spot every year?"

They nodded.

We rode our bikes back to Daddy's house. (Tia had borrowed David Michael's bike and Nancy had borrowed Linny's. Linny is Hannie's brother.) Then we played hide-and-seek in the backyard. It was easy for me to find everyone, maybe because I know my backyard so well.

I was sad when Tia and I had to go inside for dinner. And Hannie and Nancy had to go home. But it had been a perfect day.

Tia on the Farm

On Monday, Charlie drove Kristy, Tia, Hannie, and me to camp. We arrived a little early. I wanted to show Tia around the farm. Mrs. Stone met us in the driveway. So did Ollie.

I threw my arms around him. "Oh, Ollie, I missed you," I said.

Mrs. Stone held out her hand for Tia to shake. "Welcome to Farm Camp, Tia."

Tia smiled. "Thank you," she said.

Mrs. Stone told Tia about the county fair and the groups she could join. (I had already told Tia not to join the cooking group, mostly because of Mr. Pest.) Then we took Tia on a tour of the farm. Ollie followed me everywhere. He butted me, then Tia.

"He is doing that because he is hungry," I explained to Tia.

"I know," said Tia.

"We have to give him a bottle," I said. Tia watched while I fed Ollie. Then Tia and I watched the other groups so Tia could decide which one to join. (That was Mrs. Stone's idea.)

The sewing group had decided to make a baby quilt. They were busy cutting scraps of material into squares.

"Are you making the Lambie Pie quilt?" I asked Nancy.

"No, we are making the one with the baby bear on it," she said.

"Oh." I was disappointed.

Tia knew a lot about sewing. She taught the group how to make a bear. "All you need is to cut one large shape," she said. "Then you can make the muzzle, paws, and

feet separately and sew them on the body."
I could tell the sewing group really wanted
Tia in their group. But she had not seen
the other groups yet.

The cooking group let us taste their new
batch of brownies. Yuck. I made a face. The
brownies had too much salt in them.

"We are still working on this recipe,
Karen," Ricky said.

"You need to," I said.

Bobby stuck his tongue out at me.

"I told you he was a pest," I said later.
Tia nodded. We were sitting outside with
Ollie. I was sneaking him a second bottle.
We watched the produce group water their
tomato plants.

Tia liked the produce group. "There are
only three people in it," she said. "There
would be room for me."

"Wait a minute," I said. "You know a lot
about livestock, don't you?" Tia smiled.
Her parents raise lambs and pigs on their
farm. "Tia," I continued. "Why don't you
help me with Ollie? We could enter him

together." (Why had I not thought of this before?)

"I don't know, Karen," Tia said. She sounded just like Mrs. Stone and Kristy. She told me Ollie was not built like a market lamb. (That is the category the judges would put him in.) He was not long enough. His lower legs were not thick enough.

I was not listening too closely. How could I when Ollie was nuzzling my arm?

"Oh, Tia, please," I said. "We would have so much fun training Ollie together."

Tia was quiet for a moment. I could tell she was thinking. Finally, she said, "Okay, Karen, I will help you." Tia is a good friend.

I could tell the sewing and produce groups were disappointed not to have her. But I did not care. With Tia in my group, I was sure Ollie would win.

Downtown

"I think food tastes much better outside," I said. I popped another marshmallow in my mouth. Tia shrugged. But she reached for another marshmallow, too.

Camp was over for the day. Tia and I were pretending to camp out in my backyard. Charlie had even let us borrow his tent. The two of us had collected enough twigs to build a pretend bonfire. And Nannie had brought out a bag of marshmallows we could pretend to toast. (We were eating them raw instead.)

"Do you want to go wading in the brook again?" I asked.

Tia shrugged. "If you want to," she answered.

I sighed a little. Tia seemed so quiet. She never became excited about anything. She was not like this in Nebraska. I hoped she was not homesick.

"Karen, Tia!" Nannie called from the kitchen door.

"Yes," I answered.

"Would you like to go downtown with me? I have to pick up some milk."

"Downtown? Is that where the stores are?" Tia asked. She jumped up and almost knocked over the bag of marshmallows.

"Yes," I answered. "Would you like to go?"

"Sure!"

"We're coming!" I called to Nannie.

A few minutes later, we met Nannie in the driveway and climbed into her old pink car. (She calls it the Pink Clinker.)

I could not figure Tia out at all. Here we

were in a hot stuffy car. And Tia seemed so happy.

"Karen," she asked, "what does 'cinema' mean?" We were driving through downtown Stoneybrook.

"Oh, that is just Stoneybrook's movie theater," I answered.

"They are playing something called *Coppélia*."

"I have seen that movie already," I said. "It is very sad."

"Oh." Tia sounded a little disappointed. "Karen," Tia said again. (She did not even turn in her seat to look at me. Her eyes seemed glued to the window.) "What is Pizza Express like?"

"It is just a place where you can eat pizza," I said. I could not believe Tia would be interested in fast food. But she was. She wanted to know if you could see the cooks making the pizza. And what kind of toppings they had.

"Pizza! Pizza!" Emily screamed at the top

of her lungs, only it sounded more like *pia, pia.*

"Not today, Emily," Nannie answered.

When we drove by the department store, I thought Tia would jump out of her seat.

"Karen," she said. "What a huge store! What do they sell there?"

"Clothes," I answered. "And toys. And boring grown-up stuff like dishes and furniture."

"I love the clothes in the window," Tia exclaimed.

I looked at the store windows, too. I saw mannequins of little kids dressed in blue-and-white-striped dresses and pant suits. They wore straw hats with blue ribbons. Big deal.

Nannie drove into the grocery store parking lot. Tia loved the grocery store. She looked in all the aisles. "Karen, there is *so* much food here. You can even buy chocolate from Switzerland!" she exclaimed.

I gave Tia a funny look. She had never cared about fancy foods or clothes back in Nebraska. I decided Tia had changed.

11

Mrs. Stone Is Tired

Today was Tia's fourth day at Farm Camp. When we arrived in the morning, we gave Ollie his bottle right away. Then we combed and brushed him.

"Tia," I said. "Maybe Mrs. Stone would let us give Ollie a shampoo?"

"We are going to have to wash him right before the fair," she answered.

"Will we use baby shampoo?" I asked.

Tia laughed. "We need something stronger than that. At home we use Woolrite."

"Woolrite?"

"Yes," Tia explained. "It's the same stuff we use to wash wool sweaters."

"Oh," I said. I guess that made sense. "After we wash him, I am going to put bows in his wool."

Tia shrugged. "If that's what you want to do, Karen," she said. "But people don't usually put bows on livestock."

"I want to," I insisted.

"Okay," Tia answered. "But now we should see if Ollie will let us put a leash around his neck."

Ollie would not. Every time we tried, he ran away. First he ran to the vegetable garden. He walked all over the lettuce, and even nibbled some.

"Karen!" yelled Chris. "Keep Ollie away from the tomatoes. We are growing big ones for the fair."

"I am trying to." I panted. I was out of breath from chasing Ollie. "Ollie, come here." Ollie kept nibbling the lettuce. Chris lunged forward and caught him.

The next time Ollie saw his leash, he ran right into the Stones' farmhouse. Someone had left the kitchen door open by mistake. Luckily, lambs do not eat brownies. But the cooking group was not happy.

"Karen," Pamela shrieked. "Get your lamb out of here!" Pamela held a mixing bowl high above her head. She danced around the kitchen. Ollie followed her. Finally, Tia and I caught Ollie and dragged him outside. But not before Pamela gave us a mean look.

After that, the cooking group would not let us taste anything they made. (I did not care *too* much. They could keep their salty old brownies.)

We did not try to halter Ollie again that day. Instead we visited Nancy and her sewing group. They were still cutting up pieces of fabric. Nancy showed us the colors they chose for the quilt — red, green, and white.

"Don't you want brown for the bear?" I asked.

"Yes," Nancy said. "And a lot of green for the background."

As I was leaving camp that day, I bumped into Mrs. Stone.

"Oh, hello, Karen," Mrs. Stone said. "I am sorry I did not see you. I am not myself today."

"Are you sick?" I asked. Mrs. Stone did not look well. She had dark circles under her eyes. And she kept yawning.

"No, I just feel very tired. Ollie has woken me up at four in the morning for the past few days. He stands under my bedroom window *baahing*. He won't stop until I give him his bottle. I can't understand it."

Uh-oh, I thought to myself. No more extra bottles for Ollie.

A Bad Day

It was now Friday afternoon. Camp was over until Monday. That meant we would not see Ollie. Tia and I would not sing songs, play games, work in the garden, or see the other campers (except Hannie and Nancy) for three days. Boo and bullfrogs!

"I cannot believe Farm Camp is already half over," I complained to Tia. We were sitting on a bench in Daddy's garden.

Tia agreed.

"I *love* Farm Camp!" I exclaimed. "What are we going to do until Monday?"

"Could we go to the mall?" Tia asked. (I had told Tia about all the stores there.)

I raised my eyebrows. "On this beautiful day?"

Tia gave me a funny look. She looked disappointed and a little mad at the same time. Then something awful happened. Tia burst into tears.

I did not know what to do. I had never seen Tia cry before. "What is the matter?" I asked. "Are you homesick?" I touched her shoulder.

Tia sniffled and shook her head. "No, I am not homesick."

"Then what is wrong?" I handed Tia a wrinkled tissue from my pocket.

"Oh, Karen," Tia began. She blew her nose again. "It is just that when I came to visit, I was hoping to see things I cannot see at home. I do not mean to be selfish. But I can play outside anytime. And as for Farm Camp. Well, it is fun. But I *live* on a farm. I have never been to a mall or a city."

I nodded. No wonder Tia had been acting

58

strange. She was unhappy. I felt awful. "I am very sorry," I said. I promised her that the rest of her visit would be different.

Tia smiled. "Does that mean we can go to the mall?"

"Of course," I answered. "I will go find Nannie right now. Maybe she will drive us there."

I found Nannie, Daddy, and Kristy in the kitchen. I told them how Tia had been feeling. They understood right away. Best of all, they helped me plan things for us to do.

Kristy said she would walk us around the mall. (Charlie would drive us there.) She said Hannie and Nancy could come along, too.

And guess what? Daddy said he would take us to New York City. We would spend a whole Saturday there. I ran to tell Tia. She was so excited that she jumped up and down.

13

To the Mall

We're off to see the maaalll
The wonderful, wonderful mall
The mall, the mall, the mall, the mall
The wonderful place to be

I was singing the tune from *The Wizard of Oz*. But I was making up the words. It was Saturday. Tia, Kristy, Charlie, Hannie, Nancy, and I were in the Junk Bucket. And guess where we were going?

Washington Mall is far away. Charlie had

to drive almost half an hour to get there. But I kept everyone happy with my singing. Tia laughed and laughed at the songs I made up.

Finally, Charlie turned off the highway. I made sure he drove past the big white marble fountain in front of the mall. I wanted Tia to see it. The fountain shoots a spray of pink water into the air. (Tia was impressed.)

Soon we were inside the mall. Tia, Hannie, Nancy, and I ran ahead.

"Girls! Let's stay together," Kristy called.

"Okay," I said. I made Tia close her eyes. Then I took her arm and led her down the main aisle. "What do you smell?" I asked.

"Pretzels . . . donuts . . . pizza," Tia answered.

"Good!" I said. We were passing the food court. Tia opened her eyes and looked at all the stands.

"Oh, Karen, the food looks so good," she said.

My friends and I decided we were hungry.

First I ate a pretzel. Then I bought a donut with strawberry jelly inside. Yum. Tia bought a slice of pizza. Nancy bought an ice-cream cone. Hannie bought popcorn.

After we ate our snacks, we stopped at the pet store. We pressed our noses to the window to look at the kittens. Some of the kittens pressed their noses against the glass, too.

"Look at the one with gray and black stripes," Tia said.

"I like the one with the long red fur," I said.

"Boo-Boo would not be happy if we brought home another cat," Charlie reminded us.

"Oh, I do not want another cat," I said. "What would Moosie think?"

After the pet store, we took Tia to the BookCenter. The BookCenter is *the* greatest bookstore in Stoneybrook, maybe even the whole world.

Tia, Hannie, Nancy, and I walked down the aisles. We saw rows and rows of picture books. We read some to each other. (The manager lets kids do that.)

We looked at books about dolls, cats, dogs, trees, dinosaurs, and famous people. I picked up a farm book. Maybe it could tell me how lambs win blue ribbons.

"Girls," Kristy called. "There is a puppet show here today. It is about to start."

"Let's go," Nancy said.

We found seats near the stage. Actually we sat on brightly colored cushions. Guess what the show was? *Cinderella.* One of my favorite fairy tales. Tia's too. We both cried a little during the last scene when Cinderella and the prince were married. They rode away in a beautiful carriage led by four white horse puppets.

When the show was over, we clapped and clapped.

"Can we peek in the toy store?" I asked Kristy as we were leaving.

"No," said Kristy. "We do not want to be late for dinner."

I did not really care. It had been a perfect day. This time, Tia thought so, too.

14

Movie Night

Tia and I had a great week at Farm Camp. I was happy that Tia was acting like her old self. She laughed and told jokes. She also helped me with Ollie. I could now lead Ollie on a rope — most of the time. I spent every morning brushing and petting him. And I told him what a wonderful lamb he was. (Animals need to feel loved.)

Tia and I were very busy. But not too busy to sing songs, help in the garden, and visit Hannie and Nancy.

Hannie's group spent a lot of time watering their tomato plants. They were also growing zucchini and eggplants. But the tomatoes looked the best.

Nancy's group was busy sewing their squares of fabric together to make bigger squares. Soon they would be ready to sew all the squares onto the backing — the bottom layer of the quilt.

I did not visit the cooking group too much. They had never forgotten the time Ollie ran into the kitchen.

Mrs. Stone kept asking how I was doing with Ollie. "Oh, fine," I always answered.

After camp, we did what Tia wanted to do. That meant we stayed inside and watched TV or videos.

On Wednesday we had Movie Night. We made popcorn and lemonade. We invited Hannie, Nancy, and my big-house family into the TV room. Then Tia and I served the snacks. "The popcorn and lemonade are on the house," I announced.

"That means we do not have to pay for them," said Andrew.

"I know what it means, Andrew," David Michael replied.

"Quiet, please," I said. "The show is about to begin." We watched *Little Women* and everyone loved it, except Emily. She fell asleep. Tia loved the New York scenes.

"That movie took place about one hundred years ago. New York does not have low buildings like that any more," I said.

"Some neighborhoods in New York do," Daddy reminded me.

"Yes. But a lot of the buildings are tall," I said.

"As tall as the Empire State Building?" asked Tia.

"Well, no, mostly shorter," said Daddy.

That gave me an idea. "Daddy, can we go to the Empire State Building?" I asked.

"Would you like that, Tia?" Daddy said.

"Sure!"

"Okay, we will go," Daddy said. "Right to the top."

"Yippee!" I shouted.

On Friday after camp, Tia and I went to the library. We checked out some books on New York City. I showed Tia pictures of the tall buildings, the huge parks, and the gigantic department store called Macy's. "It is the world's largest store," I said.

"Everything in New York looks big," Tia said.

"It is," I agreed.

15

New York, New York

Our trip to New York began Saturday right after breakfast. Tia and I drove to the train station with Daddy. We parked the car, then stood on the platform waiting for the train to arrive.

"Toot! Toot!"

"The train is coming!" I shouted. I was very excited. I love trains.

We climbed on the train and found three seats together. Tia and I talked all the way to New York.

As the train approached the city, it went underground. We could see only darkness outside the window. Soon the train stopped with a big *screech*. "We're here!" I shouted.

We walked into Grand Central Station. Tia said it was the most crowded place she had ever seen. We all held hands. We did not want to get lost.

Out on the street, we saw many yellow cabs. Most of them were honking. Daddy hailed one. We piled into it. "The Empire State Building, please," he said.

The cab took us down Fifth Avenue. Daddy pointed out the New York Public Library. "Look at the giant lions in front," I told Tia.

Tia turned and stared at the two lion statues. "I thought you meant real lions," she said, laughing.

From the street, it is hard to tell how tall the Empire State Building really is. But from the top, it is easy. Daddy pointed out other tall buildings. "There is the United Nations, the Met Life Building, and the Chrysler Building," he said. "And there's the World Trade Center."

"The World Trade Center is taller than the Empire State Building," I told Tia.

I could have stayed on top of the Empire State Building forever. But it was getting pretty windy.

"Is anyone hungry?" Daddy asked. We were. When we were back on the sidewalk, we all bought hot dogs at a stand. They were delicious.

"Next stop, Central Park," Daddy said.

Central Park was full of people, pigeons, and trees. We followed signs to the Central Park Zoo.

Tia loved the zoo. We spent a long time watching the polar bears swim and somersault in their huge pool. Then we went into a building with a jungle inside. We saw parrots and other tropical birds.

"These birds have the brightest feathers," Tia said.

"I do not think I want to live in the jungle," I said. "It is too hot and humid."

It was not much cooler outside. But at least the seals looked cool. We watched them splash in their fountain and catch food in mid-air.

"I wish I could eat that way," I said.

Daddy and Tia laughed.

We left the zoo and walked past a pond filled with toy sailboats. "Look over there," said Daddy.

Tia gasped. In front of us was a huge bronze statue of Alice in Wonderland. She sat on a mushroom throne. Tia climbed on Alice's head. I sat on her lap.

After awhile Daddy looked at his watch.

Uh-oh. I knew what that meant. We had to catch our train.

At the station, we bought bagels and cream cheese to eat. (Daddy said that was real New York food.)

"Why do bagels have holes in the middle?" Tia asked. I giggled.

We bit into our bagels as the train pulled out of the station. "Delicious," I said.

Tia nodded. "I love New York," she added.

16

County Fair

Today is the last day of Farm Camp. Boo. But we were going to spend all day at the county fair. Yea!

The cooking group finished baking their brownies yesterday. They were decorating them to look like hamburgers. (That was Bobby's idea.) They put gobs of chocolate frosting and almonds on the top and bottom of each brownie.

"Now they look like they are in sesame seed buns," Bobby said proudly. (I did not think they looked very good.)

The produce group had their tomatoes and zucchini all ready. Their tomatoes looked very red and round. The zucchini were a little on the small side. So small that Charlotte did not want to enter them in the contest. But Chris insisted.

"Well, all right," Charlotte finally agreed. She did not sound too happy. Charlotte is one of those people who always likes to do her best.

"Karen, Tia!" Nancy called. "Come see our baby quilt."

Tia and I followed Nancy into the sewing room. The quilt looked beautiful, even if it did not have a lamb on it. In the middle was a bear sitting on the grass. (The green squares were the grass.) He was eating a pot of honey.

"It looks really great," I said. In fact, the quilt looked so good, I was even a teensy bit jealous.

"Come see Ollie," I said to Nancy. Tia and I had shampooed Ollie the day before. We had cleaned his hooves and brushed him. I had even fluffed up his wool and tied blue ribbons in it.

Nancy, Hannie, and the other campers thought he looked cute. Tia did not.

"No other lambs in the contest will be wearing bows," she said.

Why not? I wondered.

"Children, are you ready to leave?" Mrs. Stone called.

"Yes!" we yelled.

Kristy, Hannie, Nancy, Tia, and I hopped in the back of Mrs. Stone's van with Ollie. Ricky's mother drove the other campers and Mallory in her van.

It took half an hour to drive to Greenvale.

"Look!" I shouted. "A Ferris wheel. We must be here!"

We drove to the fairgrounds. Balloons were tied to the front gates.

"Karen, make sure to keep Ollie on his leash," Mrs. Stone said as we piled out of the cars.

"I will," I answered.

Inside the fairgrounds, we saw big tents

with white and yellow stripes. There were little kids carrying balloons and grown-ups in straw hats. We smelled hot dogs, cotton candy, popcorn, and French fries.

"I'm hungry," said Bobby.

"I want to go on the rides," said Ricky.

"Oh, look, there's a merry-go-round," said Hannie.

"And a little train," Chris added, pointing.

"And a sign for llama rides," I exclaimed. This fair was gigundoly cool.

17

A Royal Princess

"First you have to register for the contests," said Mrs. Stone. "After that, you may explore the fair."

Mrs. Stone asked Tia and me to wait for her. She was helping the other kids first. Boo.

"Why don't you take Ollie and look at the other animals while you wait?" Mrs. Stone suggested. "I will meet you in front of the sheep arena in half an hour." Kristy showed us where the animal arenas were.

First, Tia, Ollie, and I looked at the pigs.

We saw pink pigs and brown pigs, little pigs and big pigs, clean pigs and muddy pigs.

"Pigs roll in the mud to keep cool," Tia explained. "They will have to be washed before they enter the contest."

Next we walked to the cattle arena. The cattle were in stalls. Some ate hay. Some slept. Some flicked flies away with their tails. None of them noticed us. They did not notice Ollie either. Not even when he butted one of them. Tia and I had to drag Ollie away.

"It is time to meet Mrs. Stone and the rest of the kids," said Kristy.

As soon as we walked in the sheep arena, I gulped. The sheep looked big and sleek. They had all been shorn. And none of them had ribbons in their wool.

Mrs. Stone looked at me. "Are you sure you still want to enter Ollie in the livestock contest?" she asked.

I took a deep breath. "Yes," I said.

Mrs. Stone and I registered Ollie. Then

we settled him in his pen. I took Ollie's halter off and petted him. "I will see you later," I whispered.

"Why don't we split into small groups? That way we can explore the fair before the contests begin," Mrs. Stone suggested.

"All right!" some of the kids shouted.

Tia, Hannie, Nancy, and I were in Kristy's group. (That was good because we like to do the same things.)

First we decided to eat. Tia wanted a corn dog. I wanted cotton candy. Hannie wanted curly fries. Nancy wanted fry bread — a piece of fried dough with sugar and cinnamon sprinkled on top.

"This would be easier if you all wanted the same snack," Kristy said.

"You sound like Daddy," I told her. She laughed.

Luckily we found a stand that sold everything, except cotton candy. I had a corn dog instead. Like Tia.

"Time to go on the rides," I said when we finished eating.

"Let's not go on anything too wild," Nancy said. "Not on a full stomach, anyway."

First we went on the merry-go-round. I sat on a pink and white horse and pretended to be a royal princess visiting her country estate. I turned my nose up in the air. I waved to the crowd without bending my wrist.

When my friends and I went on llama rides. We pretended to be royal princesses.

"Your Royal Highnesses," Kristy called, "the contests are about to begin."

I crossed my fingers. Even royal princesses need good luck.

Ollie in the Ring

"Oof!" I was pulling Ollie into the ring. The livestock judging was starting. I led Ollie by his halter. Then I noticed something. None of the other sheep were wearing halters. Oops.

I quickly took off Ollie's halter and handed it to Tia. (She stood outside the ring.) Then I turned back to Ollie. But guess what. He had already run away.

"Ollie! Come here!" I shouted. Ollie ran around the ring. He butted one of the other contestants, an older girl wearing jeans and cowboy boots. Finally I caught Ollie. The girl gave me a dirty look. Some of the other kids laughed. I felt my face turn bright red.

Finally, Ollie settled down. I squatted beside him. I put one hand around his neck and the other under his chin, just like all the other kids were doing with their lambs.

Then the judge came into the ring. He was wearing jeans and a plaid shirt.

The judge asked us to lead our lambs in front of him. I noticed that he was staring at Ollie. (Maybe it was the bows.)

Guess what. Ollie would not let me lead him. He sat in the middle of the ring and would not budge. Then he ran away. The judge looked at us and shook his head. (I guess we did not do too well in that part of the contest.)

Next the judge asked us to form a line in front of him. He walked up and down each row. He checked the lambs' hind leg muscles to see how strong they were. He

checked the thickness of their lower legs. He also looked to see if they had wrinkles around their necks.

When the judge checked Ollie, Ollie reared up on his hind legs. Then he butted me.

I heard the audience giggling. The kids in the ring looked sorry for me. The judge looked kind of impatient.

The judge tried once more to check Ollie. This time Ollie ran away again. He bounded around the ring. The judge gave me a Look. I knew what it meant. I caught Ollie and led him out of the ring.

Tia helped me put Ollie in his pen. Then we sat in the bleachers with Kristy and watched the rest of the contest. Soon the judge announced the winners. I did not hear Ollie's name.

"I guess Ollie did not win anything," I said.

"No," Tia agreed. "Are you upset?"

"Not really," I said. (I was a teensy bit

embarrassed.) "You guys warned me. So did Mrs. Stone."

"Yeah," Kristy said gently.

"But you know what?" I said. "I still think Ollie was the prettiest lamb in the contest."

19

The Contests

Tia, Kristy, and I rushed to the big barn. We arrived in the middle of the cooking contest.

"Where have you guys been?" Bobby whispered loudly.

"At the livestock contest," I whispered back, just as loudly.

"Sshhh!" Pamela said frowning.

Hannie and Nancy turned around. They waved to Tia and me.

The three judges walked up and down the aisles looking at the entries. I looked too. There were cakes in all shapes and sizes. One looked just like a cow. Another was shaped like a pig. Another looked like a big red barn. And, of course, there were the brownie hamburgers.

"The entries are judged on taste and appearance," Mrs. Stone told us. (I thought the cow cake looked the best.) The judges must have thought so, too. It won a blue ribbon.

"Moo!" Bobby called out.

I groaned. Hannie rolled her eyes.

"He is acting like a sore loser because his hamburger brownies did not win," I whispered. My friends agreed.

"They are judging the produce next," Hannie told us.

We walked over to the giant zucchini, pumpkins, and eggplants.

"Wow, they must have needed a crane to lift those pumpkins," Ricky said.

"The other zucchini look so long next to ours," said Hannie.

"I told you we should not have entered ours," said Charlotte.

Soon a judge picked up a microphone and announced the results. The giant pumpkin won first place. And Hannie's group won third place for their tomatoes. The judge handed them a white ribbon. I was happy for them.

Last came the sewing contest. Two judges checked the shirts, skirts, and quilts. Hannie, Nancy, Tia, and I looked at the quilts, too. We walked slowly down each aisle.

We saw quilts with patches in the shapes of rabbits, sheep, and sailboats.

"Look, there is one with shells and starfish," cried Hannie.

"I like the one with the lamb on it best," I said. "I mean besides yours, Nancy."

The sewing group's quilt did look good. I thought it deserved to win something.

And it did. It won a red ribbon! (It came in second place.) I was proud of my friends.

We stayed at the fair for another hour. And there was a lot to see. Hannie, Nancy, Tia, Kristy, and I went to the rabbit barn. We petted the rabbits, except the ones that looked as if they might bite. Then we sat outside and watched a dance contest. The band was great, so Tia, Hannie, Nancy, and I danced, too.

Tia and I walked to the truck with Ollie. "You know what?" I said.

"What?" asked Tia.

"Ollie did not win anything. But the fair was fun, wasn't it?"

"Gigundoly fun," Tia answered.

20

Good-bye, Tia

It was Tia's last day in Stoneybrook. Daddy, Hannie, Nancy, and I were going to take her to the airport that afternoon.

After breakfast, I left Tia alone so she could pack. Besides, I had a surprise for her. When Hannie and Nancy came over, I told them about my surprise. They said they would help me with it.

We headed to my room. I had decided to make Tia a scrapbook of all the things she saw on her trip. I pulled out some old magazines.

"Here," I told my friends. "I found pictures of Central Park and the Empire State Building."

While Hannie and Nancy cut out the pictures, I drew a picture of Ollie at the fair. I pasted that in the scrapbook, along with a poem I had written about the mall.

Then Nancy and Hannie wrote Tia a letter. I found a photo of Shannon and Boo-Boo. We pasted the letter and the photo in the book, too. Finally, I wrote:

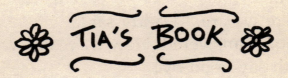

on the front cover. I tried to make the letters look extra-fancy.

"Thank you," said Tia when we gave her the present. She flipped through the book and laughed at my poem. "I had the best time visiting you."

"We left blank pages in the book," I began. "So you can add more pictures and things the next time you visit."

Tia nodded. She was trying not to cry.

Soon Daddy came upstairs to get Tia's suitcase. Tia said good-bye to everyone in my big-house family, the pets, too. Shannon licked Tia's nose.

"Who is going to get up early to feed you now, Shannon?" Daddy teased. Shannon wagged her tail.

A couple of hours later, Daddy's station wagon swung into the parking lot at the airport.

"Here we are," Daddy said.

"Boo," I answered. Now we really would have to say good-bye.

We walked Tia onto her plane. Tia had her own personal stewardess. Her name was Allison.

"Hello, Tia," Allison said. "Welcome aboard."

Tia looked at Daddy, Hannie, Nancy, and me. "Thank you for taking me to New York and Farm Camp, and for showing me all around."

96

Tia began to cry. She could not help it.

"Saying good-bye is gigundoly hard," I said. Then I began to cry, too.

Each of us hugged Tia. We made her promise to visit us again, maybe next summer.

Tia was going back to Nebraska. And Nancy, Hannie, and I were going home. We had another month of summer left.

L. GODWIN

About the Author

ANN M. MARTIN lives in New York City and loves animals, especially cats. She has two cats of her own, Gussie and Woody.

Other books by Ann M. Martin that you might enjoy are *Stage Fright*; *Me and Katie (the Pest)*; and the books in *The Baby-sitters Club* series.

Ann likes ice cream and *I Love Lucy*. And she has her own little sister, whose name is Jane.

Little Sister

Don't miss #76

KAREN'S MAGIC GARDEN

"That garden must have been *here*," Diana said, looking out the window. "They were staying in this house."

"But we explored the whole yard," I reminded her. "We did not see any magic garden."

"Maybe it is not here anymore. Or . . . was it the herb garden?"

"No." I shook my head. "This magic garden has walls around it. I did not see any walls in the yard."

"Look through the other diaries," Diana said. "Maybe Annemarie says where it is."

I was very excited. A magic garden! Right here in Lobster Cove! And it would be our secret: mine and Diana's.

"The mystery of the magic garden," I said. A shiver went down my spine.

LITTLE APPLE®

BABY SITTERS
Little Sister™

by Ann M. Martin,
author of The Baby-sitters Club ®

☐	MQ44300-3	#1	Karen's Witch	$2.95
☐	MQ44259-7	#2	Karen's Roller Skates	$2.95
☐	MQ44299-7	#3	Karen's Worst Day	$2.95
☐	MQ44264-3	#4	Karen's Kittycat Club	$2.95
☐	MQ44258-9	#5	Karen's School Picture	$2.95
☐	MQ44298-8	#6	Karen's Little Sister	$2.95
☐	MQ44257-0	#7	Karen's Birthday	$2.95
☐	MQ42670-2	#8	Karen's Haircut	$2.95
☐	MQ43652-X	#9	Karen's Sleepover	$2.95
☐	MQ43651-1	#10	Karen's Grandmothers	$2.95
☐	MQ43650-3	#11	Karen's Prize	$2.95
☐	MQ43649-X	#12	Karen's Ghost	$2.95
☐	MQ43648-1	#13	Karen's Surprise	$2.95
☐	MQ43646-5	#14	Karen's New Year	$2.95
☐	MQ43645-7	#15	Karen's in Love	$2.95
☐	MQ43644-9	#16	Karen's Goldfish	$2.95
☐	MQ43643-0	#17	Karen's Brothers	$2.95
☐	MQ43642-2	#18	Karen's Home-Run	$2.75
☐	MQ43641-4	#19	Karen's Good-Bye	$2.95
☐	MQ44823-4	#20	Karen's Carnival	$2.95
☐	MQ44824-2	#21	Karen's New Teacher	$2.95
☐	MQ44833-1	#22	Karen's Little Witch	$2.95
☐	MQ44832-3	#23	Karen's Doll	$2.95
☐	MQ44859-5	#24	Karen's School Trip	$2.95
☐	MQ44831-5	#25	Karen's Pen Pal	$2.95
☐	MQ44830-7	#26	Karen's Ducklings	$2.95
☐	MQ44829-3	#27	Karen's Big Joke	$2.95
☐	MQ44828-5	#28	Karen's Tea Party	$2.95
☐	MQ44825-0	#29	Karen's Cartwheel	$2.75
☐	MQ45645-8	#30	Karen's Kittens	$2.95
☐	MQ45646-6	#31	Karen's Bully	$2.95
☐	MQ45647-4	#32	Karen's Pumpkin Patch	$2.95
☐	MQ45648-2	#33	Karen's Secret	$2.95
☐	MQ45650-4	#34	Karen's Snow Day	$2.95
☐	MQ45652-0	#35	Karen's Doll Hospital	$2.95
☐	MQ45651-2	#36	Karen's New Friend	$2.95
☐	MQ45653-9	#37	Karen's Tuba	$2.95
☐	MQ45655-5	#38	Karen's Big Lie	$2.95
☐	MQ45654-7	#39	Karen's Wedding	$2.95
☐	MQ47040-X	#40	Karen's Newspaper	$2.95
☐	MQ47041-8	#41	Karen's School	$2.95
☐	MQ47042-6	#42	Karen's Pizza Party	$2.95
☐	MQ46912-6	#43	Karen's Toothache	$2.95

More Titles... ➡